The BEAR Who DARED

For Harry and Margaux,
may you always giggle with glee at the wonders of this world —B

Note from Author
This is just the beginning for Blue and his crew
He's off to new places and hopes you'll come along too.

Bear Affair Books
Los Angeles, California 90046 USA

Library of Congress Control Number: 2023909575
A CIP catalogue record for this book is available from the British Library.
ISBN 979-8-9870849-7-7 (hardcover)
ISBN 979-8-9870849-4-6 (paperback)
FIRST EDITION 2023

A CIP catalogue record for this book is available from the British Library.

Bear Affair Books, an imprint of Bear Affair Inc
www.bearinabowtie.com

BEAR AFFAIR
INC.

The BEAR Who DARED

Barry Brandon Waldo

Marcin Piwowarski

In a faraway forest with flowers and streams
There lived a BLUE bear with a lot of big dreams.

The place he called home was named Very Small Town.

It was full of big bears—every one of them **BROWN**.

Blue tried to fit in like he thought that he should

And practiced to be the best bear that he could.

He **SCRATCHED** his small back to avoid burping fleas

And 'BORROWED' fresh honey from bear-friendly bees.

He hid his bow tie to please **BARE**-naked fans.

He ate slimy grubs out of **SMELLY** trash cans.

He rubbed gooey mud on his **BELLY** and face

And Blue did it all with the utmost of grace.

But some of those bears
    still created a **FUSS**,
"We see your blue color—
    you're **NOT** one of us."

Those bothersome bears

walked away with a pout

And BLUE became bluer

on the inside and out.

Then one day, while gazing at clouds in the sky,

He saw a bright FLASH of blue feathers go by.

A DAZZLING blue bird, it flew into a tree.

And Blue thought, *Hmm, maybe that bird's quite like* ME.

He ran to the tree and looked up in surprise.

He scratched his small head, and he rubbed his wide eyes.

"This TREE grows from books. Its long limbs form a MAP!"

Blue summoned his courage and gave it a TAP.

Great magic awakened and golden leaves stirred.

Out peeked a suitcase in the shape of that **BIRD**!

"Hello? What's your name?" Blue called out to her nest.

"**SUE HOOT!**" chirped the owl, "And it's time for a test."

What happened next made the little bear SHRIEK.

To Blue's great surprise, the tree started to speak.

"Grab onto my branch and DISCOVER the world."

The Travel Tree swayed, and her branches unfurled.

Little Blue,

    wishing that he was much **FITTER**,

Began his long **CLIMB**

    with his nerves all a-jitter.

He passed the first branch and he let out a PUFF.

"This is HARDER than I thought," he said with a huff.

The night soon arrived, and he thought about home.

"Should I just give up? I can't do this alone."

Something tapped on his paw. It was three tiny ants.

"Bonjour, Monsieur Bleu,"
signed the **ANTS WEARING PANTS**.

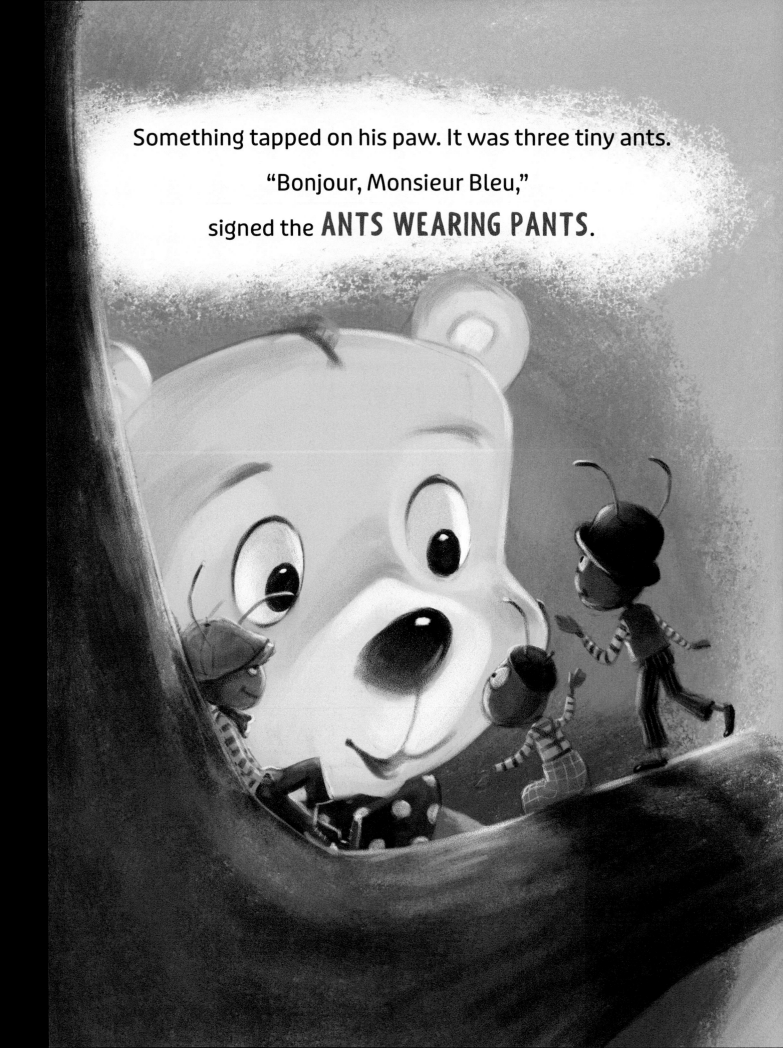

He climbed even more and met five singing bees

Who wore flowery shorts that went down past their knees.

The **BEES IN CAPRIS** sang, "Hola, we'll come too!"

"We'd like to *beeee* friends, and *beeee* part of your **CREW**."

Another branch up, something PINK brushed Blue's fur,

A cat-shaped umbrella that started to PURR.

He rubbed her soft ears and then patted her head.

"Don't stay here alone. Come and JOIN us instead."

Upward Blue pushed and when he wanted to STOP,

He climbed one last branch and he POPPED through the top.

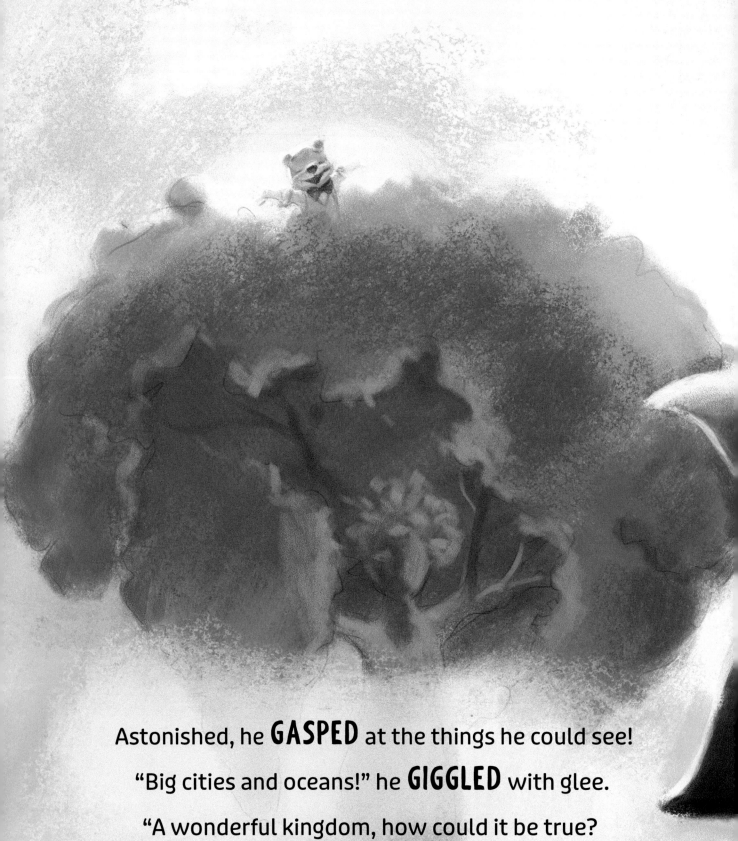

Astonished, he **GASPED** at the things he could see!

"Big cities and oceans!" he **GIGGLED** with glee.

"A wonderful kingdom, how could it be true?

And all kinds of creatures . . . and some of them blue!"

"There's **butterflies,**

lizards

and **Blue Mystery snails.**

Iguanas

and **peacocks**

and mighty **blue whales.**"

He clutched the catbrella and SOARED to the ground.

His crew of new friends were all gathered around.

"Prepare for a TRIP!" said Blue to Sue Hoot.

"I'll build a BEARPLANE while the ants map a route."

With **WOOD** from the tree

and the Bees with buzz saws,

Blue made a Bearplane

with his own handy **PAWS**.

They worked mighty hard and built all through the day
Until those gruff bears showed up **BLOCKING** their way.

They fretted and **FUMED**, "Bears don't wear bright bow ties!
We **DON'T** have blue fur and don't **FLY** in the skies.
We avoid all strange ants and don't **TALK** to the trees—
We certainly **DON'T** make friends with bees in capris!"

Now something had CHANGED
about that young blue bear.
He BELIEVED in himself
and his friends who stood there.

"The world is so BIG." Blue's voice rose to a roar.

"An assortment of colors and friends to ADORE.

A forest with LOVE needs red ants and striped bees,

A blue bear, a pink cat, and HUH-MAZING green trees."

The smallest of cubs raced and came to his aid.

That baby bear spoke up. She was not afraid.

"Who are WE to decide what this blue bear can do?

Maybe we should try being MORE ourselves too."

The Travel Tree raised him up and looked very proud,

"This **BEAR IN A BOW TIE** stands out from the crowd."

His heart was a-flutter.

Should he go?

Would he dare?

Then *WHOOOSHHHH...*

...Off he flew with the wind in his hair.

With a plane full of **FRIENDS** and his heart full of **LOVE**,

Blue circled the forest and roared from above...

"**DARE** to be your own bear in all that you do.

This world's full of magic. It's waiting for **YOU**!"

BV - #0041 - 070823 - C31 - 279/216/2 [4] - CB - 9798987084977 - Gloss Lamination